'Til Death

by Alexis Scheer

Music & Lyrics by Dan Ryan

FOR PRODUCTION INQUIRIES

UNITED STATES AND CANADA
info@concordtheatricals.com
1-866-979-0447

UNITED KINGDOM AND EUROPE
licensing@concordtheatricals.co.uk
020-7054-7298

Each title is subject to availability from Concord Theatricals Corp., depending upon country of performance. Please be aware that *'TIL DEATH* may not be licensed by Concord Theatricals Corp. in your territory. Professional and amateur producers should contact the nearest Concord Theatricals Corp. office or licensing partner to verify availability.

No one shall make any changes in this title(s) for the purpose of production. No part of this book may be reproduced, stored in a retrieval system, scanned, uploaded, or transmitted in any form, by any means, now known or yet to be invented, including mechanical, electronic, digital, photocopying, recording, videotaping, or otherwise, without the prior written permission of the publisher. No one shall share this title(s), or any part of this title(s), through any social media or file hosting websites.

For all inquiries regarding motion picture, television, online/digital and other media rights, please contact Concord Theatricals Corp.

MUSIC AND THIRD-PARTY MATERIALS USE NOTE

Licensees are solely responsible for obtaining formal written permission from copyright owners to use copyrighted music and/or other copyrighted third-party materials (e.g. artworks, logos) in the performance of this play and are strongly cautioned to do so. If no such permission is obtained by the licensee, then the licensee must use only original music and materials that the licensee owns and controls. Licensees are solely responsible and liable for clearances of all third-party copyrighted materials, including without limitation music, and shall indemnify the copyright owners of the play(s) and their licensing agent, Concord Theatricals Corp., against any costs, expenses, losses and liabilities arising from the use of such copyrighted third-party materials by licensees. For music, please contact the appropriate music licensing authority in your territory for the rights to any incidental music.

IMPORTANT BILLING AND CREDIT REQUIREMENTS

If you have obtained performance rights to this title, please refer to your licensing agreement for important billing and credit requirements.

'TIL DEATH premiered under the title *BREAKING THE STORY* and was originally commissioned and produced by Second Stage Theater (Carole Rothman, President and Artistic Director; Lisa Lawer Post, Executive Director) in New York City on June 4, 2024. The production was directed by Jo Bonney, with scenic design by Myung Hee Cho, costume design by Emilio Sosa, lighting design by Jeff Croiter, sound design by Darron L. West, projection design by Elaine J. McCarthy, hair & makeup design by J. Jared Janas, choreography by Kelly Devine, vocal coaching by Liz Hayes, original music by Dan Ryan, and casting by The Telsey Office (Karyn Casl, CSA; Destiny Lilly, CSA). The Production Stage Manager was Alfredo Macias and the Assistant Stage Manager was Genevieve F. Kersh. The cast was as follows:

MARINA . . . . Maggie Siff

BEAR . . . . Louis Ozawa

SONIA . . . . Geneva Carr

CRUZ . . . . Gabrielle Policano

GUMMY . . . . .Julie Halston

NIKKI . . . . .Tala Ashe

FED . . . . .Matthew Saldivár

UNDERSTUDIES . . . . .Laura Jordan, Jorge Luna,
Angelica Toledo, & Caris Vujcec

ACKNOWLEDGMENTS

My deepest gratitude to Carole Rothman and the very many people at Second Stage who helped develop the play there, including Jo Bonney, Maggie Siff, Sarah Lunnie, and the *Breaking the Story* team at the Tony Kiser. Additional thanks to Di Glazer; Young Playwrights Ukraine; Juliette Ojeda; the artists at the picnic tables of Interlochen and the back theatre at Boston Playwrights Theatre; and The Pickle Council: Lila Rose Kaplan, Kirsten Greenidge, Kira Rockwell, David Valdes, and Walt McGough who empowered me to keep working on the play (and restore its original title) after the first production, and reminded me that plays are never finished, they simply open.

CHARACTERS

MARINA – F. White. 40s/ 50s. A foreign correspondent for an American news channel. Fiercely competent on the field, but unable to keep a firm grip at home. Elegant, Sharp, and Absolutely Fucking Losing It.

BEAR – M. 40s/50s. A cameraman for an American news channel. Marina's fiancé. Rugged, Charming, and True to His Vows.

SONIA – F. 40s/50s. Marina's Maid of Honor. A socialite and philanthropist. Cold, Meticulous, and Ready For Battle.

CRUZ – F. Latina. 20s. Marina and Fed's daughter. A singer/songwriter and almost college senior. Gifted, Resilient, and Writing a Song.

GUMMY – F. White. 60s/70s. Marina's mother. A retiree. Funny, Blunt, and Letting Go.

Also appears as a **REFUGEE** – Disturbed, Tender, and Looking for Her Daughter.

NIKKI – F. 30s. A freelance journalist and Marina's colleague. Cunning, Ambitious, and Here For The Inside Scoop.

Also appears as the **AID WORKER**.

FED – M. Latino. Late 40s/Early 50s. Marina's ex-husband. An anchor for an American news channel. Suave, Romantic, and Here To Win Her Back.

Also appears as the **MAN**.

*Non-speaking roles that appear in the intrusions of war, including **MAN** and **AID WORKER** can be played by additional ensemble members. The role of **REFUGEE** should always be doubled by the actor playing **GUMMY**.

SETTING

A lovely place to throw a garden wedding in Wellesley, Massachusetts.

Also, a War Zone.

TIME

Right now. Or in the near future. Or maybe it already happened.

NOTES ON PRODUCTION

A forward slash [/] indicates the point of interruption in overlapping dialogue.

Text in between double less than/greater than signs [**<< >>**] indicates a heightened state of being, and a slippery grip on reality. These are intrusions of war on Marina's psyche. Maybe they're realized through video projections. Maybe there's an ensemble. Or maybe it's just sound and lights. Think of it as a texture or filter that is being added to distort the world of the Wellesley garden.

When French was spoken in the play we did *not* use supertitles. When Ukrainian and Russian were spoken we *did* use supertitles.

AUTHOR'S NOTES

In the fall of 2019, I picked up the book that inspired me to write this play, *In Extremis: The Life of War Correspondent Marie Colvin* by Lindsey Hilsum. At the time, my boyfriend Dan (now husband) was in the middle of chemotherapy treatment for Stage IV small bowel cancer, and we were speaking the ill-fitting language of war as he waged this great *fight*, this great *battle* in private. It seems obvious to me now, all these years later, that I picked up that biography and dozens after it because I was looking for the courage to stare at this terrible thing head on and not lose hope. And who better to draw strength and inspiration from than those who have dedicated their lives to bearing witness? I wrote the play and Dan wrote music for it during the years he cautiously journeyed towards survivorship, through a pandemic and multiple wars breaking out – we spent our honeymoon in a hotel in Montreal watching Russia invade Ukraine – the balance of life and death always feeling so immediate. Writing this note feels scary and exposing, like the first official public documentation of the scars we both carry; Dan's, of course, more significant and literal. But it feels necessary to mention because that experience is what lies underneath the play. To be clear, this is not a play about cancer. But it is about the kind of psychic reckoning I hope we're all afforded with our loved ones as we face our own mortality. It's both a requiem and my own *The Wizard of Oz* in a way. A call home. To rest. To peace.

"Hasta la muerte, todo es vida."
– Cervantes

For my husband, Dan.
Dayenu.

(In the dark, the sounds of war are muted and distorted by post-explosion ringing.)

*(A faint light picks up **MARINA**, who wears a helmet and bulletproof press vest. She's disoriented, trying to shut the ringing out.)*

MARINA. This is a nightmare. **THIS IS A FUCKING NIGHTMARE.**

<<

(An explosion of breaking news and angry girl rock. **MARINA** *disappears from view as* **CRUZ**, *her daughter, bursts out with a microphone and sings her viral song "Yesterday's Revolution." It feels like a music video.)*

CRUZ.
TWO, THREE, FOUR!
CHOOSE SOMEONE ELSE TO BLAME
HATE DROWNS ME, SET IT ALL AFLAME
THIS TOWN, MY TOWN! IT ALL BURNT DOWN
IN YESTERDAY'S REVOLUTION

(War rages around her.)

THE STORY THAT YOU NEVER LEARNED
WHEN I WAS YOUNG EMBERS STILL BURN
THIS HEART, MY HEART, IT RIPPED APART
IN YESTERDAY'S REVOLUTION

---

* A license to produce *'Til Death* does not include a license to publicly display any third-party or copyrighted images or text. Licensees must acquire rights for any copyrighted media or create their own.

(The 24-hour news cycle appears like a hurricane.)

CRUZ.

THERE'S NO HAPPY ENDING,
SO LET'S JUST STOP PRETENDING
I WANNA FEEL THE FLAME, RECLAIM, PROCLAIM
SET FIRE TO MY NAME, AND WATCH IT BURN

(On the word "burn" a breaking news headline appears: **RUSSIAN AIRSTRIKE HITS HOSPITAL***)*

WATCH IT BURN
WATCH IT BURN

(Screamed.)

FUCK!

(War continues to rage.)

I HEAR ALL YOUR EMPTY WORDS
THEIR VACANT WEIGHT, THE BURDEN HEARD
THIS MIND, MY MIND! WAS TRAPPED, CONFINED
IN YESTERDAY'S REVOLUTION

(Breaking news headline: **RUSSIA CLAIMS HOSPITAL WAS LEGITIMATE TARGET***.)*

BRICKS, STONES THROWN, WALLS PUNCHED OUT
THIS ENDLESS SHIT, ALL AROUND
THIS HOUSE, MY HOUSE! WAS HOLLOWED OUT
IN YESTERDAY'S REVOLUTION

THERE'S NO HAPPY ENDING,
SO LET'S JUST STOP PRETENDING
I WANNA FEEL THE FLAME, RECLAIM, PROCLAIM
SET FIRE TO MY NAME, AND WATCH IT BURN

(On the word "burn" a breaking news headline appears: **AMERICAN JOURNALIST MARINA REYES MISSING, PRESUMED DEAD***.)*

WATCH IT BURN
WATCH IT BURN
WATCH IT BURN
WATCH IT BURN
WATCH IT BURN

   *(**CRUZ** breathes heavily as if she has just won a physical fight.)*

   (The song ends, thrusting us into darkness.)

   >>

   (And then suddenly…)

   *(**MARINA** appears in a gorgeously green garden in the backyard of a home in Wellesley, Massachusetts.)*

   *(**BEAR** joins her with a cup of coffee, smoking a cigarette.)*

MARINA. Heaven, right?

BEAR. *(He loves it.)* I hate it.

MARINA. Don't ask how much it cost.

BEAR. I can't believe you bought a house.

MARINA. *(Giddy.)* Neither can I. Listen.

BEAR. What?

MARINA. It's so quiet I can hear all my intrusive thoughts!

BEAR. That's what I'm saying! I'm just so fucking sad! Here! I'm sad here!

MARINA. Do you wanna go to a hotel? You could be sad at the Marriott?

BEAR. I'd feel less ridiculous.

MARINA. But you wouldn't smell as good.

BEAR. I used the two hundred dollar cream on your dresser. / I googled it.

MARINA. You goo– you asshole! Well, you're glowing.

BEAR. I gotta be honest, this is not what I was expecting.

MARINA. You thought I lived in some abandoned apartment. Mail piled up. Old takeout in the fridge.

BEAR. That's me you're describing. But no, really, how much was this place? Five? Six mil?

MARINA. I said don't ask.

BEAR. I can –

MARINA. Don't google it!

BEAR. I can't believe you bought a house here. When are you ever in Massachusetts?

MARINA. Don't say Massachusetts like that.

BEAR. *(Even more annoying.)* Massachusetts.

MARINA. And it's not just Massachusetts. It's Wellesley. Or as my mom would say, *Swellesley.* She used to bring me here to go Trick or Treating. I always told her I'd live here one day.

And now look – this year it's gonna be *me* with the carved pumpkins. Full-sized candy bars. Tombstones on the lawn. Ghosts dangling from the trees, blowing in the wind.

      (**BEAR** *pulls out his phone.*)

BEAR. I'm googling it.

MARINA. No! Stop! Just enjoy it!

BEAR. *(Whiny.)* It's all too much. The gold leaf invitations, the black car, the roses, this house. And then tomorrow you're gonna make me wear a suit so some rich people can give you an award, and then I'm gonna have to schmooze and I hate schmoozing.

MARINA. You're performing disgust, but deep down I think you're into all this. You just don't wanna lose your street cred.

BEAR. No really, these award things freak me out. They like reinforce this hierarchy of suffering and make it feel like we're all competing to break and capture whatever terrible thing is at the top. It's some real thirty-pieces-of-silver shit.

MARINA. Is that why you keep your Emmy in a drawer?

BEAR. Yeah. I hate that thing.

MARINA. But you deserved it. What you went through to get that footage home.

BEAR. *(Facetious.)* That's exactly what I was thinking when I was kidnapped, "Now at least I might win an Emmy!"

MARINA. You've never talked about Libya.

BEAR. It's history.

MARINA. Only if it's recorded.

BEAR. Not much to put on record.

MARINA. All the other guys did interviews.

BEAR. I don't like the spotlight.

MARINA. They turned that one guy's book into a movie.

BEAR. It tanked.

MARINA. You could have written a book, a book they turned into a movie.

BEAR. *(Sharper than intended.)* I was handcuffed to a chair for sixteen days! Nobody wants to see that!

MARINA. *(Disarming him.)* I guess bondage is off the table for us then.

BEAR. *(Relaxing again.)* I didn't say that.

MARINA. Well, I'm looking forward to this award thing for once. It'll probably be my last.

BEAR. What do you mean?

MARINA. I'm retiring. Wow that's weird to say out loud. I'm retiring. *(To the garden.)* I'M RETIRING!

BEAR. You're kidding.

MARINA. I'm announcing it tomorrow. It's part of my acceptance speech.

BEAR. Holy shit.

MARINA. Distinguished Achievement. It's like they wanna give me a Lifetime Achievement Award in case I die out there next time, but they don't want to be obvious about it.

BEAR. Glad to know that's the consolation prize for having a missile land on your head.

MARINA. But you were there too. *(Overdramatic.)* Why am I alone in the misfortune of being recognized?

BEAR. You're more interesting than me.

MARINA. It's 'cause I'm a woman and they think I'm fragile.

BEAR. No one thinks you're fragile.

MARINA. Then damaged. But the sexy kind of damaged that makes me still appealing.

BEAR. Admit you love the attention.

MARINA. *(A deadly smile.)* I'm a weapon of mass contradiction.

BEAR. Retirement. Fuck.

MARINA. Can you believe it?

BEAR. Twenty years on the front line.

MARINA. And I've got the scars to prove it.

BEAR. What are you gonna do next?

MARINA. You're looking at it. I'll soak in the tub for the next century. Get a dog. Maybe write a book.

BEAR. A book they'll turn into a movie?

MARINA. And I'll be with Cruz for once. I mean honestly, I just wanted to get her out of the dorms. Make sure she's okay. *(At a loss.)* I don't know, all she does is sleep.

BEAR. And write. I heard her working on a song last night.

MARINA. She's been locked in her room ever since I got back.

BEAR. She just needs time.

> (**MARINA** *can't shake a bad feeling.*)

Hey, it's not your fault.

> (**BEAR** *brings her in for a hug or kiss. He melts away her bad feeling.*)

MARINA. It's weird having you here. All clean and calm in my pretty green garden.

BEAR. Should I go?

MARINA. No.

BEAR. Good.

MARINA. Do you ever think what your next chapter looks like?

BEAR. *(A lie.)* No.

MARINA. *(Coy.)* Bear, why are you here?

BEAR. You invited me.

MARINA. And?

BEAR. And – and I wanted to see if this was real. If this could be more than the off-on work spouse thing we've been doing for years.

MARINA. And? What's the verdict? Is it real?

BEAR. If you want it to be.

MARINA. *(Smiles.)* I gotta warn you. I'm a War Zone Ten. But a Real World Three. Four on a good day.

BEAR. I've seen you shit in a bucket, Marina.

MARINA. It gets worse.

BEAR. I already know you talk in your sleep.

MARINA. I do?

BEAR. Sometimes. When you're having a nightmare.

MARINA. What do I say?

BEAR. You're calling out for Yasmin.

MARINA. The Sapphire.

BEAR. The hotel bombing, I know. Legendary coverage.

MARINA. What else do I say?

BEAR. *(Matter of fact.)* "I'm bleeding. I'm bleeding."

MARINA. I'm bleeding?

BEAR. The hospital strike?

> (**MARINA** *doesn't remember bleeding after the hospital attack, but she doesn't dwell on it.*)

MARINA. Well, it bleeds it leads I guess. Don't worry, Sonia – my friend Sonia, she'll be here soon – she'll drag me to some spa – that usually helps the nightmares. You know, realign my chakras, touch grass, smell the flowers. Oh! You should know this about me: I hate roses.

BEAR. No roses.

MARINA. They remind me of my ex. Everything warranted roses. A casual lunch. Roses. A minor disagreement. Roses. Picture our wedding.

BEAR. Roses.

MARINA. It was beyond.

BEAR. So you don't like weddings.

MARINA. Oh no, the wedding was awesome. It was the marriage that sucked.

BEAR. Would you get married again?

MARINA. Like in general, or to you?

BEAR. In general.

MARINA. No. Not in general. But I could marry you, I think.

BEAR. *(Pulling her in close.)* Oh, really?

MARINA. I do have a very strict no-fucking-off-the-field rule. *(She kisses him.)* And we've broken that. *(Kisses him.)* A few times. *(Kisses him.)* So now we have to get married. I don't want all the other correspondents thinking I'm so easily won.

BEAR. Of course.

MARINA. Let's get married.

BEAR. Everyone's right, you are crazy.

MARINA. Probably. So what?

BEAR. You're funny.

MARINA. You want me, come and have me.

BEAR. Hold on, hold on. I might be a War Zone Ten. But I'm a Real World Five.

MARINA. You're a War Zone Eight.

BEAR. Heeeey!

MARINA. Marry me.

BEAR. You're serious.

MARINA. What, are you scared?

BEAR. Me? Scared? Never.

MARINA. Then?

BEAR. Okay. Okay! Let's do it! Let's get married!

> *(A knock on a glass door somewhere in the distance.)*

MARINA. This weekend, let's do it this weekend!

BEAR. So soon?

MARINA. Everyone's already coming for the award tomorrow, we'll just tack it / on the day after.

BEAR. Just tack it on?

MARINA. We have the house, the yard.

BEAR. But –

> *(More knocking.)*

MARINA. That must be Sonia.

BEAR. What do I wear?

MARINA. Whatever you want, it's your wedding!

> *(The knocking grows in intensity.)*

I need to get that.

BEAR. What?

MARINA. The door!

BEAR. Marina –

MARINA. GET THE FUCKING DOOR!

>>*War breaks through the door. It rolls through the garden like a wave, setting* **MARINA** *off balance, and then leaves.*<<

(Time blinks forward.)

*(**SONIA** is on the phone. **BEAR** and **MARINA** mix mimosas.)*

SONIA. Well of course there's enough space and chairs and tables – the furniture will be mismatched, but that's very in right now. China. Silverware. Glassware. Linens. Oh, call the woman who did the flowers for the gala, her husband's being indicted and I wanna throw that poor woman a bone. Catering is set. *(To* **MARINA.***)* Do you have a dress?

MARINA. No.

SONIA. *(On the phone.)* No. She is hopelessly committed to that hideous little capsule wardrobe. Would probably get married in cargo pants and a tunic if I let her.

MARINA. I would!

SONIA. *(On the phone.)* I'll call Michele. *(To* **MARINA.***)* I need your measurements. *(On the phone.)* Flowers, food, clothes, what am I forgetting? OH. Music. Put on the new assistant. This will be a project for her. What's her name? Ashley. *(To Ashley.)* Ashley! I have a special project for you because you're young and from the art world. I need a string quartet. Or a rock band. It doesn't matter which, surprise me. I'll take anyone who isn't booked Sunday.

Yes, the day after tomorrow.

No, I'm not kidding – I know, I know.

(A friendly glare to **MARINA***, comforting a clearly overwhelmed assistant on the phone.)*

SONIA. I didn't realize I'd be planning a wedding in a weekend either, but what do I always say? "Anything is possible if you're *im*possible." I want high maintenance. I want stubborn. I want unreasonable. And I know you can bring the waterworks, because I plucked you out of Drama School myself. And remember, bribery and blackmail are not beneath us. I believe in you. Now put Rachel back on. Thank you, sweetie. *(To Rachel.)* Rachel? If she doesn't have a band booked by the end of the day I want you to fire her. I'll talk to you later. *(She hangs up the phone.)*

BEAR. Have you ever considered running for office?

SONIA. No. I actually like getting things done.

MARINA. *(To* **BEAR.***)* You wouldn't like her politics.

SONIA. Bear. Bear. Do you have a normal name?

MARINA. It's –

BEAR. Bear! Please! Everyone calls me Bear!

SONIA. Bear. Bear. Bear.

MARINA. This is crazy, right?

SONIA. Fine line between true love and insanity.

MARINA. But the wedding – it's not too much?

SONIA. It's an intimate elopement.

MARINA. Is it eloping if my mom comes?

SONIA. To elope is to escape. And here we are in this understated suburban escape. It's going to be beautiful. Leave it to me.

MARINA. *(Hugging her soul sister.)* I love you.

SONIA. But I'm billing you for my assistant's overtime.

　　　*(***BEAR** *chokes on his mimosa.)*

No, Marina, don't tell me you're broke.

MARINA. *(Smacking* **BEAR***'s arm.)* I'm not broke!

SONIA. How could you be broke?

(**BEAR** *gestures broadly.)*

SONIA. The house? This is your – you bought this house?

MARINA. Did you think we were squatting?

SONIA. I thought it was a little weekend rental.

BEAR. Don't ask how much it cost.

SONIA. Oh my god.

MARINA. You knew I wanted to come back.

SONIA. To Wellesley? Why?

MARINA. It's home.

SONIA. You're from Framingham. The shitty part.

(Drinks her mimosa.)

What about you, Bear? Where are you from?

BEAR. I'm a citizen of the world.

SONIA. Oh I love that. Me too.

MARINA. She's from Long Island. The shitty part.

SONIA. I speak four languages.

BEAR. Five.

MARINA. Six. I win.

BEAR. No you don't.

MARINA. Yes I do.

BEAR. *(Counts.)* English, French, Italian, Russian, and conversational Arabic.

MARINA. Spanish.

BEAR. Marina *Reyes*, how could I forget? You won that Latin media award cause they didn't know Reyes was your ex-husband's name.

MARINA. I know, I need my own affinity group for white women with diverse last names. It's a tricky time for us.

BEAR. *(TV voice.)* "Fernando Reyes. The Reyes Report."

MARINA. He's a good guy.

BEAR. Must be if you kept his name.

SONIA. I'm sure you're a good guy too, Bear.

BEAR. War Zone Eight. Real World Five.

SONIA. Well, you convinced her to retire. That makes you a Ten to me.

MARINA. He didn't convince me.

SONIA. We've all been trying to talk her into it for years.

MARINA. It was my decision.

SONIA. I was gonna come and watch her accept her award and then bribe her to stay in the States. But now look! We're planning a wedding! *(To* **MARINA.***)* And then you can move back to New York!

MARINA. I'm staying here.

SONIA. Where?

MARINA. Here. In my house.

SONIA. It's a vacation house.

MARINA. Except I'm gonna live here when I'm not on vacation.

SONIA. *(Ew.)* No. Why?

MARINA. Cruz.

SONIA. Cruz can come to New York. What's here?

MARINA. *(Bliss.)* Nothing.

SONIA. Are you okay with this?

BEAR. She needs the quiet.

SONIA. *(Like **MARINA***'s not there.)* How's she doing?

MARINA. I'm right here.

BEAR. You saw her when you walked in. Sweaty, shaky, white as a ghost.

SONIA. And the nightmares?

BEAR. She's screaming in her sleep.

SONIA. It's always something. The bombing, the kidnapping, the thing in Syria. I really don't know how you people keep going back. Trauma on trauma on trauma.

BEAR. It's what we do.

SONIA. You sound just like her.

MARINA. Nope! Not anymore! I've changed my tune!

SONIA. *(Finally acknowledging her.)* OH MY GOD, we haven't talked about Cruz's new song!

MARINA. What new song?

SONIA. The one that went viral.

MARINA. *(So confused.)* What?

SONIA. Where is Cruz?

MARINA. Locked in her room.

BEAR. She's writing.

MARINA. She's depressed.

BEAR. Give her a break.

MARINA. She had a song go viral?

SONIA. Have you been living under a rock?

MARINA. Just a War Zone.

BEAR. I knew about it.

MARINA. You did??

BEAR. *(Duh.)* Yeah, it went viral.

    *(**CRUZ** enters eating a waffle.)*

CRUZ. Are you talking about me?

MARINA. She has risen!

    *(**SONIA** rushes to **CRUZ** and gives her a massive hug.)*

SONIA. CRUUUUUZ!!!

CRUZ. Hiiiiiiiiiiii.

BEAR. I'll give you guys girl time.

    *(**BEAR** heads off.)*

SONIA. Your mom says you're a shut-in – you've gone all Emily Dickinson on us!

CRUZ. Oh my god, she's so dramatic!

SONIA. Are you okay?

CRUZ. I'm working on my new EP.

SONIA. I think that's a symptom of depression.

CRUZ. *(Genuinely.)* I'm not depressed!

    *(**SONIA**'s phone rings.)*

SONIA. Excuse me.

    (She answers the phone in French.)

Michele! My friend, how are you? I'm calling to ask you for a small favor. And I just want to remind you that you owe me. Are you sitting down?

(**SONIA** *excuses herself to take the call in private.*)

CRUZ. What are you telling people about me?

MARINA. Nothing! And Sonia's not people. Sonia's Sonia.

CRUZ. I'm just...working some shit out. Like you. Except I have a healthier outlet.

MARINA. What does that mean?

CRUZ. I'm writing music. You? You bought a midlife crisis mansion.

MARINA. I'm not having a midlife crisis.

(**SONIA** *comes back in.*)

SONIA. I need a rapid fire decision. White, Ivory, or Champagne?

(**MARINA** *tops off their drinks.*)

MARINA. Ivory for the dress! Champagne for us!

SONIA. *(On the phone in French.) Ivory.*

(To **MARINA**.*)* What about shape and material?

MARINA. I want my boobs to look good. I don't want to itch. And I gotta be able to shake my ass.

(**SONIA** *rolls her eyes.*)

SONIA. *(On the phone in French.) Think simple. Classic. Elegant.* This is an older bride.

MARINA. Hey!

CRUZ. *(Counting.)* Midlife crisis mansion, midlife crisis marriage.

SONIA. *(On the phone in French.) That's it! You are brilliant, my friend! Thank you! Thank you! Bye! (Hangs up.)* What did I miss?

MARINA. Cruz is gonna play me her song that went viral.

CRUZ. No I wasn't.

SONIA. Yes!! Play!!

MARINA. Play!!

SONIA & MARINA. Play! Play! Play! Play! Play! Play!

> (**CRUZ** *begrudgingly pulls out her phone.* **MARINA** *and* **SONIA** *go wild.*)

SONIA.	**MARINA.**
PLAAAAYYYYYY!!!	AHHHHHHH!!!!

> *(Time blinks forward.)*

SONIA. *(To* **MARINA,** *deliciously.)* Isn't it dark?! *(To* **CRUZ.***)* Tell her about the trend!

CRUZ. People are using my song for these transition videos where they start in their like PJs with no makeup and then on the "watch it burn" it cuts to them in like a sexy outfit.

SONIA. They're fabulous!

> *(Singing.)*
> WATCH IT BURN!

CRUZ. Mom?

> …

> What do you think?

MARINA. *(Unsettled.)* It's – I don't know – familiar?

CRUZ. Dad was cleaning out some boxes and we found / your old journals.

MARINA. My old journals.

SONIA. What is this? What's happening?

CRUZ. I've been using them for inspiration. *(Tender.)* Is that okay?

MARINA. Why does your dad still have those?

CRUZ. The estate planner guy said they're an asset. They're gonna release all your unpublished writing when you die.

MARINA. Right. Of course.

CRUZ. Is it okay, Mom?

> (**MARINA** *wants to say "it makes me feel naked, but I'm proud of you" but can't.)*

MARINA. Yeah. *(Laughs unexpectedly.)* It's weird, but sure.

> *(Everyone lightens up.)*

CRUZ. I'll list you as one of the writers so you're cut into royalties if you're pressed about the intellectual property.

MARINA. No! Stop! My god, listen to you, "royalties" and "intellectual property." *(To* **SONIA**.*)* Can you believe this is my daughter!?

SONIA. Believe me, I can.

MARINA. I bet your roommate is thrilled you're moving off campus. She'll finally have some peace and quiet.

CRUZ. *(Evasive.)* Yeah.

MARINA. Did you get into Susan's lecture class this semester? Do you want me to email her?

CRUZ. We can talk about it later.

MARINA. What? No! What else are we doing?

CRUZ. Please, later. After the wedding.

> (**SONIA** *knows the conversation* **CRUZ** *is trying to dodge and tries to help her.)*

SONIA. Oh! I have to show you the gala photos!

(*She pulls out her phone.*)

MARINA. I saw them.

SONIA. No, the professional ones. They just came back.

MARINA. (*To* **CRUZ**.) Are you changing your major?

CRUZ. Stop.

SONIA. Look how beautiful she looks!

MARINA. Cruz?

SONIA. Her making her speech.

CRUZ. Mom, look at the photos!

SONIA. Making her speech again.

MARINA. You're changing your major.

SONIA. Those were the centerpieces.

MARINA. You're allowed to change your major.

CRUZ. Oh my god.

SONIA. Her and Gummy.

MARINA. Really!

SONIA. Her and her dad.

MARINA. Cruz, honey, you're not gonna hurt our feelings by deciding you don't want to be a journalist. There are so many other things you can do!

SONIA. Me and her.

MARINA. Poli-sci, International Relations –

CRUZ. IT'S NOT ABOUT MY MAJOR.

MARINA. Then what is it?

(**CRUZ** *looks to* **SONIA** *for support.*)

SONIA. Now's not the time.

MARINA. Do you know what she's talking about?

...

...

Just say it!

CRUZ. *(Confident.)* I'm dropping out.

MARINA. What?

CRUZ. I'm dropping out of school.

MARINA. You're two semesters away from graduating.

CRUZ. Tyler wants us to go on tour.

MARINA. Who's Tyler? I don't know Tyler.

CRUZ. We write together. He produces my songs.

MARINA. Is he your boyfriend?

CRUZ. No! He's my bandmate –

MARINA. You don't have a band!

CRUZ. Mom!

SONIA. It's just a gap year!

MARINA. No, a gap year is what you do before you start college. Not when you're about to finish it.

CRUZ. I've already made up my mind.

MARINA. This should have been a conversation.

CRUZ. Well you're not really around for conversations, are you, Mom?

(That burns.)

(A car honks in the distance.)

CRUZ. That's Gummy –

MARINA. This is punishment, right? You're punishing me?

CRUZ. This isn't about you!

MARINA. Then what is it?

CRUZ. *(Desperate.)* I just need a break!

MARINA. A break from what?

CRUZ. It's too hard.

MARINA. Too hard?!

CRUZ. Don't do that –

MARINA. TOO HARD? Do you know how good you have it? Do you? DO YOU?

        <<

        (War thrusts **MARINA** *into the middle of a chaotic scene.)*

        *(***GUMMY***, appearing as a Refugee, walks slowly, shellshocked and devastated, carrying a small bag.)*

        *(***MARINA*** reports.)*

Jim, we're here on the southeastern outskirts of the city where this small suburb has been under heavy bombardment for over a week. And what you're seeing right now is a steady stream of people who are making their way to where it is relatively safer and easier to access the aid that is so desperately needed by many. The streets have been mangled by airstrikes, debris is everywhere, and bombed out cars and tanks block so many of the roads which means people have no choice but to flee on foot. We're seeing lots of children, elderly people with mobility issues, people carrying household items and pets. And the look on everyone's face as they pass is a look of distress, but it's important for us to remember, they are the lucky ones here in this town.

GUMMY. *(In Ukrainian.) My bag, my bag.*

MARINA. *(In Russian.) Stay right there.*

GUMMY. *(In Ukrainian.) I cannot carry my bag over.*

MARINA. *(In Russian.) Please let me help you.*

(Back to the camera.) I'm just gonna help this woman with her bag, excuse me, Jim.

> *(**MARINA** takes her bag and gives her an arm to hold on to as **GUMMY** navigates the terrain.)*

GUMMY. *(In Russian.) Thank you. Thank you.*

MARINA. *(In Russian.) Tell me please, what can you tell the world about what is happening here?*

GUMMY. *(In Ukrainian.) I'm looking for my daughter. Please. I can't find my daughter.*

> *(She hugs **MARINA** tightly.)*

> \>\>

MARINA. Mom.

> *(**GUMMY** releases **MARINA** from her embrace and examines her. She is comedic relief and she knows it and relishes in it.)*

GUMMY. With a headline like "Missing, Presumed Dead" I thought you'd look worse.

MARINA. Thanks.

GUMMY. You know the Secretary of State blocked my number. Got so sick of hearing from me.

CRUZ. He blocked you 'cause you asked him out.

GUMMY. Shoot me.

MARINA. Don't worry, I already yelled at the network for that headline.

GUMMY. I coulda had a heart attack. *(Looking around.)* I might still have a heart attack. Did you see this place?

MARINA. I did. It's my house.

GUMMY. *Swellesley.* Aren't you fancy?

SONIA. Gummy, you look great!

(**SONIA** *hugs* **GUMMY**.)

GUMMY. Mmm, Sonia, you always smell so good. *(Smells again.)* Have you smelled her?

CRUZ. That's the sweet smell of gun manufacturing and private prisons.

SONIA & GUMMY. No politics.

CRUZ. Why? 'Cause your politics suck?

GUMMY. Why don't you have any lawn furniture?

MARINA. It hasn't been delivered yet.

GUMMY. Did you go to Jordan's?

MARINA. No, I hired a designer.

GUMMY. We can go to Jordan's this weekend. Or Bob's. And we're right by Bernie & Phyl's. Not tomorrow, 'cause tomorrow you have your award thing and I'm getting my hair done. But the day after we can go.

MARINA. ...We have plans? ...I'm getting married?

GUMMY. Yeah, yeah in the afternoon, but we could go in the morning.

(**BEAR** *enters.*)

BEAR. Look who I found lurking.

(**NIKKI** *enters with a smile and a wave.*)

NIKKI. Hi, hi not lurking just using the bathroom, sorry, this is not how I wanted to descend upon you this weekend but Vogue sent me to cover the wedding.

MARINA. Vogue?

NIKKI. I know. Me? Vogue?

MARINA. How does Vogue know I'm getting married?

SONIA. *(Bad at lying.)* What a mystery!

(**NIKKI** *makes herself at home.*)

NIKKI. Anyway, I was already gonna be in town for the award thing tomorrow so it totally worked out, and I wasn't planning on coming by tonight, but total coincidence, I'm at Logan and guess who out of all the people in the world I'm standing next to in line at Enterprise – Gummy! – and we started talking and she's like, "You look so familiar where do I know you from?" and I told her I'm a foreign correspondent so you probably recognize me from TV and she was like, "Oh maybe you know my daughter Marina Reyes," and I was like oh my god Marina Reyes is your daughter? Marina Reyes is kinda like my mentor and that's why I'm here for the award thing and the wedding which is probably why you're here and then I was like wait wait wait YOU'RE Marina Reyes' mother?? You're Gummy?? You are a legend!! And she's like, "Hey only my family calls me Gummy," and I'm like I know I know it's what Cruz called you when she was a baby – *(To* **CRUZ***.)* Hi – 'cause she couldn't say grandma but hear me out Marina started this thing out in the field she calls a Gummy Situation and it's when things get really bleak and she breaks out into this big Boston accent to lift the mood like, "I'm wicked pissed 'cause the cah broke down and I left my pocketbook at home so I don't even have my smokes," or or we're driving to a refugee camp or a security checkpoint and she's like, "We got time for a Dunkin' run?" I swear it is so so funny anyway we're chatting up a storm in this line and we start talking about the wedding and I'm like what happened to our most sacred rule of no-fucking-off-the-field I'm kidding I'm kidding no seriously stop I'm so happy for you two anyway long story short I talked her out of renting a car and said it would be my pleasure, I can drop you off, no worries, and here we are!

MARINA. Hi, Nikki.

NIKKI. I can leave. This looks like a family thing. Am I intruding? Will you tell me if I'm intruding?

GUMMY. Course not, the more the merrier!

BEAR. Yeah, too many normal people. I was starting to feel outnumbered.

NIKKI. *(To* **MARINA**.*)* Really, I can leave. Tell me to fuck off and I'll see you tomorrow.

MARINA. It's fine, Nikki. *(To everyone else.)* Just know we're all on the record now.

NIKKI. *(Clarifying.)* No, you're not. This is all off the record!

(Time blinks forward.)

*(***NIKKI** *has a recording device out. We're clearly on the record now, which* **SONIA** *and* **GUMMY** *love.* **CRUZ** *is noodling on her guitar and writing in her notebook.)*

SONIA. We were supposed to spend the whole summer after graduation backpacking in Europe together, but she got that internship at the Globe and well... More French boys for me!

NIKKI. Is that why she started working abroad? She got jealous?

MARINA. I've told you this story.

NIKKI. Alternative perspectives, babe.

GUMMY. No, it wasn't the boys. *(Proud.)* It was 9/11 that brought her out there.

MARINA. Told you.

CRUZ. Bush did 9/11. Can that be in the article?

SONIA. Don't believe everything you see on the internet.

CRUZ. You know there's a website that tells me how much you donate to Republicans every year?

BEAR. *(Still can't believe it.)* A *Vogue* feature.

NIKKI. I knooooow. Can I pitch you my title?

BEAR. Shoot.

NIKKI. *'Til Death: A Vow To The Front Line And Each Other.*

MARINA. Sexy!

BEAR. Except she's retiring.

NIKKI. Oh my god!? Really??

MARINA. The end of an era.

NIKKI. Holy shit, that changes everything.

(**MARINA** *stands up.*)

MARINA. Okay, what are we feeling? There's a good Mediterranean place. We could do sushi. Thai.

BEAR. I was gonna cook.

MARINA. Since when do you cook?

BEAR. It's a new level you unlock when you marry me.

MARINA. Ooo! *(To **NIKKI**.)* That's good! Write that down!

(**BEAR** *and* **MARINA** *leave.*)

(**CRUZ** *strums a new chord progression on her guitar.*)

(**NIKKI** *puts away her recorder and approaches* **CRUZ**.)

NIKKI. Okay you have to know that I'm OBSESSED with your single. I'm like full American Idol in the shower with it.

CRUZ. Oh my god, thank you!?! Sorry, I'm still not used to people like knowing me.

NIKKI. I totally get it.

CRUZ. *(Blushing.)* Yeah.

NIKKI. Are you majoring in music?

CRUZ. Journalism. But! I'm dropping out to go on tour.

NIKKI. Hell yeah!

CRUZ. I think my mom's gonna disown me.

NIKKI. Let me talk to her. My brother actually went to Berklee to play piano for a few semesters. The joke there was that if you made it all the way to graduation then you weren't talented enough to make it in the industry.

CRUZ. Does he still play?

NIKKI. No.

CRUZ. Oh.

NIKKI. No! Sorry! I mean, he's a producer now! Has a Grammy and everything.

CRUZ. Oh my god!

NIKKI. I know, can you believe I am the less successful sibling? Wait, Cruz. I should totally connect you two.

CRUZ. Seriously?

NIKKI. Yeah! Gimme your phone, I'll literally do it right now.

(**CRUZ** *hands* **NIKKI** *her phone.)*

CRUZ. Wow wow wow I cannot thank you enough. And okay, not to be a total fangirl, but I follow you on everything and I love your content. I love how you can take a piece of news that's super complicated and boil it down to like a super understandable thirty-second clip.

NIKKI. Thank you!

CRUZ. My parents think it's the death of journalism.

NIKKI. What was it like – kid of two journalists? Dad in the studio. Mom always abroad.

CRUZ. Well, I'm definitely keeping my therapist in business.

NIKKI. Sorry, I should clarify, this isn't for *Vogue*, this is just me asking.

CRUZ. You want kids?

NIKKI. I don't know. I'm freezing my eggs soon. Trying to buy more time to figure it out.

CRUZ. ...It's not easy. It won't be easy.

(In another part of the garden **SONIA** *and* **GUMMY** *gossip.)*

GUMMY. So much for your little intervention.

SONIA. I'm relieved! This weekend can just be about coming together and celebrating, and we don't have to deal with all that drama.

GUMMY. *(A big smile.)* I think we're being delusional.

SONIA. Nooo!

GUMMY. She says she's retiring, but give it a few weeks... Bear will go back to the field, she'll get bored, start drinking –

SONIA. She's already started drinking. Wait! No no no no. This, this time is different. I mean she has never uttered the word "retirement" before. Right? So, so something has changed. Something has shifted.

GUMMY. But will it last?

SONIA. She bought the house. She's getting married. And Cruz. I know she's worried about Cruz.

GUMMY. You're not convinced either.

SONIA. ...

There's this little voice inside of me. This little voice...

> (**MARINA** *appears on the other side of the garden and watches them while she downs her drink.*)

GUMMY. Bear asked for my blessing to get married.

SONIA. Did you give it to him?

GUMMY. Sure. It doesn't cost me anything.

> (*Time blinks forward.*)

> (*It's golden hour. Everyone is together again in the garden, and they are mid-conversation.* **NIKKI** *is teaching* **BEAR** *how to use her film camera.* **MARINA** *is on edge and continues to drink in an effort to soften herself [not a winning strategy].*)

MARINA. I don't believe in Feminine Intuition.

CRUZ. I do.

GUMMY. So do I!

SONIA. (*Focused on her phone.*) I'm adding seasonal linens. Everyone loves seasonal linens.

BEAR. I want a juicer.

NIKKI. I'm with Marina. Intuition isn't a psychic ability, it's just a way of processing information.

MARINA. Exactly!

GUMMY. But aren't there things you can just sense?

MARINA. Of course, but I don't think that's some divine Feminine superpower.

CRUZ. Woah woah woah! What happened to us being *(Mocking.)* "the granddaughters of the witches they couldn't burn"?

GUMMY. Who you calling a witch?

(The flash of the camera.)

NIKKI. *(Mock reporter voice.)* We're live in Wellesley, Massachusetts where award winning *female* war correspondent Marina Reyes is receiving the award for Distinguished Achievement in Conflict Journalism. Marina, who are you wearing tonight?

MARINA. *(Playing along.)* Calvin Kalashnikov.

NIKKI. And what is your secret weapon beauty product?

MARINA. Right now I'm loving Makeup by Martyrdom's Blush Bomb in Desert Rose.

BEAR. Now blow us a kiss!

(The flash of the camera.)

SONIA. Bear, come – apparently I can't intuit which juicer you want.

GUMMY. I've always trusted my gut. It's connected to the part of my body that reminds me to eat, so clearly it's trying to keep me alive.

CRUZ. *(To **MARINA**.)* You should get an Easy Bake Oven.

MARINA. Didn't I get you one of those for your birthday?

SONIA. I got her one for her birthday.

MARINA. Right, of course, Godmother of the century over here.

SONIA. I *intuited* that she wanted one.

(The flash of the camera.)

MARINA. Okay, look, what I was trying to say is that I hate how my gender is used as a qualifier. Like with the hospital strike. My instinct didn't get me and Bear to safety. My *feminine* instinct did. I'm not a war correspondent. I'm a *female* war correspondent.

CRUZ. Says the woman who wore the "future is female" sweatshirt all of twenty-sixteen.

MARINA. *(Caught.)* Okay, well, we were very young then and obviously that sentiment didn't prove to be true.

SONIA. I didn't see an ice bucket inside, did you?

MARINA. Sonia, stop! A registry is so tacky – we don't need anything!

SONIA. You need a pasta maker.

MARINA. *(Sharp.)* I need you to stop looking at your phone and be here with me!

*(**SONIA** puts her phone down.)*

SONIA. *(Fights to keep calm.)* I believe in Feminine Intuition. I know it exists because I have it. What you and Bear just went through, I knew it was gonna happen. I knew when you called me to say it wasn't "that bad" but I could hear shelling in the distance. I knew when the Americans and Brits started pulling their crews out and you stayed behind with the local journalists. And I knew when I called the Secretary of State and the best thing he could say to me was, "I'm praying for you."

MARINA. You keep repeating, "I knew." But what did you know?

SONIA. That you could have died out there!

MARINA. That's always been true!

SONIA. WELL YOU REALLY FUCKING SCARED THE SHIT OUT OF ME THIS TIME AND I JUST NEED YOU TO ACKNOWLEDGE THAT.

CRUZ. *(Soft.)* Don't bother, she can't.

MARINA. *(That hurts.)* I'm sorry. I'm sorry. Okay? I'M SORRY! I'M SORRY! I'M SORRY MY JOB IS SO HARD FOR YOU ALL!

<<

(War swirls around **MARINA** *like an angry tempest.)*

IS THAT WHAT YOU WANT TO HEAR? I'M SORRY? WELL I AM! I'M SORRY. I'M SORRY. I'M SORRY. I'M SORRY. I'M SORRY.

*(***MARINA*** *reorients herself.* **BEAR** *and* **NIKKI** *are the only ones with her now, still in the world of war.)*

NIKKI. Civilians.

BEAR. They don't get it.

NIKKI. Sometimes I think if they got a little taste...

BEAR. A little brush...

MARINA. Hey...civil war doesn't feel so far away.

BEAR & NIKKI. What would be the story?

(They delight in this game.)

MARINA. The violent seizure of our government.

NIKKI. Land battles in Pennsylvania.

BEAR. Michigan.

MARINA. North Carolina.

NIKKI. Americans illegally crossing into Mexico.

BEAR. Foreign military intervention.

NIKKI. Refugee camps.

BEAR. Internment camps.

NIKKI. We'd have bounties on our heads.

MARINA. If we still had heads.

NIKKI. Don't worry, you're retired. You'll still have a head.

MARINA. Oh, so you got this covered?

NIKKI. Learned from the best, didn't I? You'll get to be safe here, sealed up in your *Swellesley* tomb.

MARINA. I feel like you're burying me alive.

NIKKI. But you'd get to be with Cruz.

MARINA. Oh no, Cruz is probably dead in this scenario. College campuses will be both targets and hotbeds for terrorism. And come on, safe? Here? Are you kidding me? Boston would be a front line. We've got all that concentrated intelligence. Hospitals, pharmaceutical companies, biotech. The kids designing bombs and rockets at MIT. Those robo-cop dogs at Boston Dynamics – we'll finally figure out what side *they're* on. Harvard will turn into ground zero, Fenway Park a military staging ground. But see I think the mistake everyone is gonna make is underestimating how ready Boston is to fight back. I mean can you think of a place with more grit and endurance, a people united by their singular culture? The Marathon, the Sox, clam chowder, GBH, The Jimmy Fund, fucking *winter*. And all of this, ALL of this sitting on top of the bones of our Revolutionaries! I mean that's *poetry*!! Our local militia is gonna co-opt the Patriots branding and we're gonna take to the streets in our Pats gear, I swear! Boston will be a front line!

>>

(**MARINA** *is alone.*)

NIKKI. Your house is beautiful.

(**NIKKI** *has appeared unexpectedly.*)

MARINA. Thank you.

NIKKI. My parents used to bring me and my brother to estate sales every weekend, so I feel like I can really appreciate a beautiful house.

MARINA. Thanks, Nikki.

NIKKI. They collect old Hollywood memorabilia – my parents – I think it's how they hold their adopted American identity. And you know LA, a person dies and nine times out of ten they've got a crate full of old screeners and a stack of vintage movie posters collecting dust in the garage. Anyway, going to those things always made me think about the story a house tells about a person. What inspires them. Turns them on. Brings them peace.

MARINA. And what story is my house telling?

NIKKI. Honestly, that's what's confusing. I don't see you in your house.

MARINA. What do you see?

NIKKI. A showroom. The illusion of a life.

MARINA. I hired a decorator.

NIKKI. Did you tell them you've been all over the world? 'Cause I think they missed the memo.

MARINA. Well I'll make sure I pick up a rug or a woven fucking basket at the next War Zone gift shop.

(You could cut the tension with a knife.)

Vogue.

NIKKI. *Vogue.*

MARINA. I knew you were still doing domestic stuff, but really? *Vogue?*

NIKKI. You're an interesting subject. Tragic hero searches for her happily ever after.

MARINA. What about that guy in Spokane I connected you to?

NIKKI. The 4chan Hitler wannabe? No, I turned that interview down.

MARINA. He leads a major domestic extremist group. It's a great opportunity.

NIKKI. To give him a platform? Give him more oxygen?

MARINA. To push back at him! See this is where we fundamentally disagree about what our job is.

NIKKI. I know. I've been reading through your old work, back when you did print.

MARINA. I've interviewed a lot of people.

NIKKI. You put a lot of fucked-up people on the map.

MARINA. You're missing a lot of nuance.

NIKKI. Am I?

MARINA. See this? I hate this. Don't fucking do this to me in *Vogue.*

NIKKI. What?

MARINA. Flatten me in a way that makes me unlikable. "The woman gave a megaphone to fascists and dictators, has a neutral press gone too far?"

NIKKI. I didn't / say that.

MARINA. When I think that the public should know what these monsters think or else how will anyone fight against them? Like what happens when 4chan Hitler runs for elected office?

NIKKI. He'd only be running because that interview would have galvanized his supporters AND the opposition! I mean come ON the Democrats foam at the mouth for these batshit viral clickbait Republicans because they know they can fundraise off them. "Vote for us, because have you heard what fucked-up shit the other side said?!" And then that fucked-up shit becomes mainstream. And this is how we got caught in this vicious cycle, because you think by platforming these monsters you'll be able to hang them with their own words, but all you do is give them more power. More reach.

MARINA. It's our job to tell the whole story, Nikki! Not just the part of the story we agree with! I mean this is why news rooms are a mess right now, because you think every story has to fortify your echo chamber. But that's not journalism, that's activism. And look, if that's the kind of work you want to be doing, then do that, because we need activists. But don't walk around with the word "press" emblazoned on your chest pretending you're after the whole truth.

NIKKI. Objectivity is a myth.

MARINA. It's not a myth, it's a pursuit! We represent facts and ask questions so that people can make up their own mind. Balance. Fairness. Accuracy. All perspectives. The whole story.

...

NIKKI. I gave Cruz my brother's number. He's a music producer.

MARINA. What?

NIKKI. Give her some *perspective* on touring.

MARINA. I've given you my last clean pair of underwear in the field and this is how you repay me?

(*Nikki's phone rings.*)

NIKKI. (*Excited and surprised.*) Sorry, Tom's calling me –

MARINA. Why is my producer calling you?

NIKKI. (*Answers the phone with a smile.*) Tom, where are you? The party's in Boston!

(**NIKKI** *heads off as* **CRUZ** *comes back outside with her notebook, focused on a thought.*)

CRUZ. What rhymes with bone?

MARINA. Uhh...moan, loan, atone – do you want me to google it?

CRUZ. No, I'm exercising my brain.

MARINA. Flown, thrown, grown –

CRUZ. Oh, I like throne.

(**CRUZ** *writes.*)

MARINA. Cruz, I need to talk to your dad about this tour thing / before you –

CRUZ. It's fine.

MARINA. No, we're gonna talk about it –

CRUZ. We don't need to. I'm not going. What rhymes with trade?

MARINA. Made, fade, raid –

CRUZ. Stayed, paid –

MARINA. I'm not against the idea, I just think the timing –

CRUZ. I talked to Nikki's brother. He thinks touring is premature and that I should focus on writing and building a fanbase on social first.

MARINA. Are you disappointed?

CRUZ. No, I think it's good advice. He like actually gets it. Fucking Tyler has no idea what he's talking about. I'm so done with him.

MARINA. Is that what you're working on? Your post-Tyler era?

CRUZ. Yeah, I guess so.

MARINA. You know breakup albums are the best.

CRUZ. Tyler's not my boyfriend.

MARINA. You're turning red!

CRUZ. I don't wanna talk about this with you!

MARINA. Why? We never talk about this kind of stuff!

CRUZ. Exactly! It's weird!

MARINA. Come on! Pretend I'm not your mom. Pretend we're just friends.

CRUZ. *(Bold.)* Tyler and I had sex once. Last year.

MARINA. Did you use protection?!

CRUZ. You're not being a cool friend.

MARINA. Yes I am! A cool friend is asking you if you used protection!

CRUZ. Okay, maybe like question five. But the first question should be, how was it?

MARINA. I don't want to know.

CRUZ. Exactly Mom! 'Cause we're not friends! I don't ask how your sex life is!

MARINA. It's good.

CRUZ. Great! I'm so happy for you!

MARINA. I don't know what to say!

CRUZ. Oh my god, please Mom, just stop talking!

    ...

MARINA. Does this mean you're staying in school?

CRUZ. No.

MARINA. Cruz –

CRUZ. I'm taking a semester off. Maybe the whole year.

MARINA. To do what?

CRUZ. *(Truly at a loss.)* I don't know, Mom, I don't know. Get my head above water.

MARINA. Cruz, you're scaring the shit out of me. Do you need to go to a doctor?

CRUZ. No! I'm okay. I'm gonna be okay. Why don't you trust me?

    (Time jumps forward.)

    (Morning. A cake tasting for breakfast! **MARINA, BEAR, GUMMY,** *and* **SONIA.***)*

GUMMY. Why couldn't you have an engagement first?

BEAR. For the record, I did suggest that.

MARINA. What's the point of an engagement?

SONIA. To plan a wedding.

GUMMY. You don't even have a ring.

SONIA. I'm on it.

MARINA. You are?

GUMMY. It's just not very romantic. *(To* **BEAR.***)* I'm not blaming you.

MARINA. I think this is very romantic.

> *(**MARINA**, **BEAR**, and **GUMMY** all dig into a piece of cake. The taste sends an uncomfortable chill up **MARINA**'s spine.)*

GUMMY. Mmm... I love this one.

SONIA. *(Reading the menu.)* That is...

SONIA & MARINA. Coconut. Jinx.

BEAR. You don't like it.

MARINA. Blegh!

GUMMY. What? You always loved coconut! What kind of cake did you and Fed have?

SONIA & MARINA. Guava. Jinx again.

GUMMY. Riiiight. I knew it was something tropical. God, I'm having déjà vu. Picking out cake.

> *(She tries another cake.)*

This one's boring.

BEAR. *(To **SONIA**.)* You're not trying them?

SONIA. I'm not a cake person.

MARINA. She has no sweet tooth. Talk about a red flag.

SONIA. *(Proud.)* We had tiers of cheese at my wedding.

GUMMY. Bear, why isn't your family coming?

MARINA. Mom!

GUMMY. It's a reasonable question.

BEAR. Don't have much of a relationship with my parents. Big army family, so my dishonorable discharge didn't go over well. I have a son who's five and lives in London, but I didn't invite him 'cause he's five and his mom's fucking crazy. And well, that's all I got.

MARINA. *(To* **BEAR** *re: cake.)* Wait, try this one.

GUMMY. Is that why you want to get married? To be part of a family?

BEAR. *(Trying the cake.)* Oh fuck yeah.

GUMMY. 'Cause you're always welcome to visit me. I can show you off to all my boyfriends!

SONIA. Gummy!!

MARINA. Oh my god, you're unbelievable.

GUMMY. What? You shipped me off to Florida, what did you expect?

MARINA. *(To* **BEAR.***)* This is not just Florida. She was like this my whole life. A revolving fucking door.

GUMMY. I'm a free spirit!

MARINA. Nobody wants to hear about your boyfriends Mom!

SONIA.	**BEAR.**
No no, wait, I do! I do!	No, I definitely do!

GUMMY. Well, there's Robert. He's my buddy at the pool. His tan is borderline melanoma, but he is sexy. Then Jimmy, who takes me to the casino on Tuesdays and Thursdays so I can get my steps in. Mike lives on my floor, so he's really just a matter of convenience. But if I had the chance, I would have brought Richard.

SONIA.	**BEAR.**
Oooooo Richard!	Richard!

GUMMY. He's a widower. And his whole family lives in Miami, so they're always coming up to visit. They take us out to lunch. To the mall. It's a very nice family.

MARINA. I promise to visit more.

GUMMY. Come visit period. You can't promise to visit more when you've never come to visit.

MARINA. *(Re: cake.)* Try this one.

GUMMY. Oh, I brought your baby pictures.

MARINA. For what?

GUMMY. To keep here in your house.

(*She takes a bite.*)

MARINA. *(Annoyed.)* Did you bring my yearbooks too?

GUMMY. No, those are heavy. *(Re: cake.)* This is my favorite.

SONIA. Which one is it?

GUMMY. The chocolate.

MARINA. Why don't you want my baby pictures?

GUMMY. I was spring cleaning.

SONIA. Chocolate isn't very bridal.

MARINA. And you decided to get rid of my baby pictures?

SONIA. Who has a chocolate wedding cake?

BEAR. Said the woman with the cheese.

GUMMY. I'm not getting rid of them. I'm keeping them here. One less thing you need to deal with when I die. I saw it on TV. Swedish Death Cleaning.

BEAR. Wait I wanna see these pictures.

GUMMY. Do you want more kids?

BEAR. *(Looking to **MARINA** for backup.)* Uhh...

(**MARINA** *remembers something.*)

SONIA. Please, god, no.

GUMMY. You could adopt.

BEAR. I already have a kid I hardly see.

SONIA. *(To **MARINA**.)* Don't tell me you're considering this.

MARINA. There was this man at the Polish border. This man with a baby.

>><<*A* **MAN** *appears with a baby.*>>

His wife was killed the day before and now he was being conscripted. We watched him hand his infant to an aid worker at the border, then turn around to go home.

<<*The* **MAN** *hands his baby to an* **AID WORKER.**>>

GUMMY. What happened to the baby?

MARINA. I don't know. The man was killed an hour later when they bombed the humanitarian corridor, but I don't know what happened to the baby. I was gonna follow up – I was gonna visit the resettlement camp – I was gonna –

<<*The* **MAN**, **AID WORKER**, *and baby are gone.*>>

(Time blinks backwards.)

(A cake tasting for breakfast! **SONIA**, **GUMMY**, *and* **BEAR** *don't acknowledge* **MARINA**, *but* **MARINA** *doesn't catch on immediately. She's starting to get antsy.)*

GUMMY. Why couldn't you have an engagement first?

BEAR. For the record, I did suggest that.

GUMMY. She doesn't even have a ring.

SONIA. I'm on it!

GUMMY. It's just not very romantic. *(To* **BEAR**.*)* I'm not blaming you, Bear.

MARINA. I'm having déjà vu.

(**MARINA**, **BEAR**, *and* **GUMMY** *dig into a piece of cake.*)

GUMMY. *(Re: cake.)* This one is disgusting.

SONIA. *(Reading the menu.)* That is...

SONIA & MARINA. Guava.

MARINA. Jinx.

GUMMY. No it's not.

SONIA. That's what it says.

GUMMY. I love guava. She had a guava cake when she married Fed. Delicious. This is not guava.

SONIA. Well, we're in Massachusetts.

BEAR. We should get a Boston cream pie.

SONIA. Absolutely not.

MARINA. Why not?

GUMMY. Why couldn't you get married in Florida?

BEAR. The award thing.

SONIA. The intervention.

MARINA. What?

GUMMY. Right, right. The two-for-one special.

MARINA & BEAR. What intervention?

SONIA. Don't worry, it's off!

GUMMY. For now!

SONIA. But I swear, if I get so much as a whiff of her entertaining the idea of going back out there – *(To* **BEAR**.*)* Look, I'm not expecting you to be on our side, but I do expect you to stay out of the way.

BEAR. Got it.

MARINA. Bear!

GUMMY. Then when do you leave?

BEAR. Next week.

MARINA. So soon?

GUMMY. What about a honeymoon?

MARINA. The spa? My chakras?

BEAR. In the middle of a war?

GUMMY. There's always a war. People get married during war. They have birthdays and babies. *(Eats cake.)*

BEAR. We'll go another time.

SONIA. *(Re: cake.)* What's the verdict?

GUMMY. Too sweet. But wait, no, don't rush back.

BEAR. Nikki has a lead on a story, said she'd share it with me.

MARINA. Excuse me?

BEAR. Don't tell Marina.

MARINA. Are you fucking kidding me?

SONIA. Trouble in paradise.

BEAR. I still have a job to do. I have to point my camera at someone.

GUMMY. *(Loves this.)* Is Nikki her arch nemesis?

MARINA. No!

BEAR. She'd never admit it.

SONIA. Ooo I loooove the drama!

GUMMY. *(Re: cake.)* And I loooove this one.

MARINA. I don't have an issue with Nikki!

BEAR. *(Re: cake.)* Oh fuck yeah, this one's it.

MARINA. Really!

BEAR. Sonia, it's my wedding. You have to at least try it.

MARINA. *(Vicious.)* It's just that Nikki is a kid who did ONE report for *Vice*, won a fucking Peabody, got millions of followers, and NOW SHE THINKS SHE CAN TAKE MY PARTNER AWAY FROM ME? TAKE MY PRODUCER? MY JOB? SHE THINKS SHE CAN BE ME? SHE THINKS SHE CAN DO WHAT I DO?

(Time blinks backwards.)

(A cake tasting for breakfast! **MARINA** *is trying to hold on for dear life.)*

GUMMY. This one is disgusting.

SONIA. That is… *(Reading the menu.)* Guantanamo Bay. It's supposed to go with the sparkling Central Intelligence.

BEAR. Which one is this?

SONIA. The Dark Cheney.

MARINA. Chocolate.

GUMMY. That one's my favorite.

SONIA. You could pair it with a red blend. A grenade maybe?

MARINA. Grenache.

BEAR. What about this one?

SONIA. That's… Rum Ramallah. Or Rum Reuters? *(Searching on the menu.)* Rum –

MARINA. Raisin.

SONIA. Russia. That's Rum Russia.

BEAR. Oh I hate Russians.

MARINA. Raisins!

BEAR. Whose idea was it to put them in a cake?

GUMMY. Dark Cheney. I vote the Dark Cheney.

SONIA. Also keep in mind we're having Squid-Pro-Quo as the main course.

(**BEAR** *takes the menu.*)

BEAR. Look at all the ISIS flavors.

MARINA. Ice cream!

BEAR. Salted Security Council, Strawberry Two State, Kremlin and Cream...

GUMMY. There used to be this great shop around the corner from our old place. They had this Cherry Hezbollah made with French Ayatollah. Oh my god. I wonder if it's still open.

BEAR. *(Still reading the menu.)* Key Lime Spy, Peanut Butter Haram, Joint Churros, Havana Pudding, Sapphire Bonbons...

MARINA. SAPPHIRE BOMBING!

<<

(*An explosion shakes* **MARINA.** *It's followed by an alarm.* **MARINA** *quickly puts on her flak jacket and helmet, and starts speaking into the microphone and towards the camera as soon as she's able to.*)

(*The sound of sirens and shouting.*)

We're across the street from the Sapphire Hotel which was attacked by a suicide bomber just moments ago. This is where I've been staying with my crew and teams from several other news organizations for the last few weeks. At this point it's too early to know who orchestrated the attack and who their intended target was. I was here at this local café when the blast occurred. The explosion threw me from my seat, shattered all the windows, toppled tables and chairs, just to give you a sense of the impact felt here on the ground. As you can see, it's a chaotic scene. Emergency responders are working to rescue people from the hotel. It looks like many are walking out with what look like minimal injuries, but here you can see...

(**MARINA** *watches a body get carried off in a stretcher. It makes her stomach drop.*)

Yasmin? YASMIN?!? YASMIN!!!

(*She remembers the broadcast and tries to compose herself.*)

Yasmin's father, Ahmed, is the receptionist here at the hotel. She brought me my newspaper this morning. She was only here today because it's her father's birthday. I don't know where he is and if he's –

These are people. Real people. With lives and loved ones just like you and me. They wake up every morning, go to work or school, and hope to come home safe every night just like you. I don't know why I get to go home and Yasmin doesn't. I don't know.

(**CRUZ** *appears like a beacon. A strange angel in the middle of war. She sings. She accompanies herself on guitar or with a looper. Or she sings to the sounds of war.*)

CRUZ.
OH WHAT SHALL I GIVE TO THE GOD OF WAR
I'VE NO WINE, NOR GOATS, OR GOLD
WHAT SHALL I LEAVE UPON HIS ALTAR
FOR A DROP OF MY BLOOD HE'LL MAKE ME GROW BOLD
AMEN, AMEN, MAY OUR OFFERING BE RECEIVED
AMEN, AMEN, MAY OUR OFFERING BE RECEIVED

(**CRUZ** *has led* **MARINA** *to* **BEAR**. **CRUZ** *disappears.*)

> (**BEAR** *is also dressed for a War Zone. He smokes a cigarette.*)

BEAR. You were shouting in your sleep again.

MARINA. The Sapphire.

BEAR. I know. Legendary coverage.

MARINA. ...Right.

> (*Fireworks start to go off far in the distance. They're barely audible.*)

Are those...?

BEAR. Fireworks. At the Country Club. Guess we're not the only ones getting married.

> (**MARINA** *can't quite tell if she's still in Wellesley.*)

You don't belong here, Marina.

MARINA. I'm not sure I know where "here" is anymore.

BEAR. *(Having fun with her.)* You're like this sacred artifact I've stolen from the temple and now this ancient monster curse has been unleashed until I put you back. And I only have 'til the stroke of midnight until you disintegrate and the whole world turns to ash.

MARINA. *(Laughs.)* What?

BEAR. Those are the rules!

> (*His kisses her.*)

MARINA. I can't believe we're getting married.

BEAR. Cold feet?

MARINA. No.

BEAR. Good.

MARINA. I just don't know what kind of wife you're expecting me to be.

BEAR. You know the moment I fell in love with you?

MARINA. Don't tell me, don't tell me – that layover in Frankfurt?

BEAR. No. Before that. The thing in Syria.

MARINA. Oh *god*.

BEAR. *(Excited.)* We were being shot at. They hit the Canadian kid and you're screaming at me to go help him, so I double back, scoop him up, get him inside, try to patch him up and stop the bleeding, and I turn around to look at you and realize you've been hit too. But you're cool as a cucumber, making yourself your own tourniquet with your Hermès scarf. I thought, "My god I fucking love this woman."

MARINA. *(Proud.)* War Zone Ten.

BEAR. But you don't have to be that anymore. You'll show me other parts of you to love.

MARINA. What if there aren't any?

(**BEAR** *considers this.*)

BEAR. Your family would kill me if I let you go back out. Sonia would hire a hitman, but I think Gummy would do it with her bare hands.

MARINA. *(She knew it.)* You don't want me to retire.

BEAR. Don't listen to me, I'm a bad influence.

MARINA. You said I needed the quiet.

BEAR. Sure, let Sonia take you to that spa. Lay in the grass. Fatten up. But then what? You're gonna stare at the wallpaper the rest of your life?

MARINA. *(Laughs in disbelief.)* Yeah! I'm gonna meander along the luscious lawns of this sprawling New England estate picking up dog shit while you and the world spin forward without me.

(She hates how that sounds.)

BEAR. What do you want, Marina?

MARINA. Another drink.

(The fireworks start to grow in intensity.)

BEAR. What do you want, Marina?

MARINA. Another smoke.

BEAR. What do you want, Marina?

*(**MARINA** turns away from **BEAR**.)*

MARINA. *(Explosive, intoxicating.)* To go back! Every fiber in my being wants to be back over there, at the center, at the heart, where everything feels so alive and in focus. I want it! I want it so bad! I have to go back! I have to go back! I have to go back! I have to go back! I have to! I have to! I have to go home! I have to go home! I have to go home! I have to go home!

*(An explosion shakes **MARINA**. She turns around and **BEAR** is gone.)*

*(**NIKKI** rushes on to where **BEAR** was just standing. She is also dressed for a War Zone.)*

NIKKI. The entrance collapsed. They're shelling the alley.

MARINA. Nikki?

NIKKI. We're kettled in.

*(The fireworks sound like intermittent gunfire. **NIKKI** is freaking the fuck out.)*

MARINA. Hey, hey. It's okay. Breathe. A Gummy situation right? It's like the Pops at the Hatch Shell out there.

NIKKI. Sorry, I'm freezing my eggs next week and it's these fucking hormones.

MARINA. *(Lost between worlds.)* What?

NIKKI. *(Falling apart.)* I'm just exhausted! And I've been trying to keep it all together because this is your weekend and I do not take it lightly that I get to be here with you in this moment. And even though I'm pretty sure you hate me, I need you to know that I think the world of you, Marina. Like I can't even begin to explain how important you are to me and this industry. Even though we disagree on some pretty big things, I really recognize and honor the path you've blazed for women in the field. And what I think I'm trying to say is: I didn't come here to undo you. The *Vogue* feature. Or whatever comes after it. You can trust me. I don't think you're a monster.

MARINA. I do.

NIKKI. You're not.

MARINA. I've made monstrous decisions in my life.

NIKKI. Not everyone thinks that.

MARINA. *(Cheeky.)* Who's your source?

NIKKI. Yasmin.

> *(There's no more gunfire.)*

MARINA. *(Surprised.)* What?

NIKKI. From The Sapphire? Did you know she survived?

MARINA. I – (Didn't know.)

NIKKI. She has your picture hanging in her home. Says you're her guardian angel. That you spoke her name into the world and the thoughts of a million strangers saved her life.

MARINA. ...

Don't do that.

NIKKI. What?

MARINA. Don't romanticize it.

NIKKI. I'm not – it's important work –

MARINA. I don't think anyone should do what we do.

NIKKI. You don't believe that. I've seen you speak – to college students, on panels – you've said the only job security in the media industry is in war coverage. And you, you exemplify why war coverage matters. Why we need people on the front line armed only with a camera and a pen!

MARINA. It comes at a cost, Nikki!

NIKKI. I'm not saying it doesn't.

MARINA. When you've buried as many friends as I have you'll understand.

...

I don't know if I believe in guardian angels. But if they are real I guess I owe an apology to the one watching over me.

She's had to spend my whole life floating around on some cloud screaming, "What the fuck, lady?! Do you want to be blown to pieces? Do you want to get kidnapped or tortured or molested or beheaded? These are not normal things to consider!!! Why can't you just go home??!! Please!! To the two hundred dollar face cream. Heated marble floors. Get a dog! Grow a garden! Just green! Everywhere! Life!"

...

Why can't I just listen?

> *(Without* **MARINA** *realizing,* **BEAR** *has joined her and* **NIKKI**. *They seem to be mid-conversation. They're all drinking.* **MARINA** *has to reorient herself.)*

BEAR. The White House will keep imposing sanctions, but I don't think they'll deploy troops. That's not this administration's agenda.

NIKKI. But the U.S. has to support NATO, the President knows that.

BEAR. Well if we do get boots on the ground I'm gonna try and get embedded.

>   (**NIKKI** *makes a barf sound.*)

I'm not saying embeds are perfect, but it's combat experience and access that your whole class, your generation of journalists will probably never get and the work is gonna suffer.

NIKKI. What about Afghanistan? Your work suffered because you were embedded. All the news was us versus them. Our guys. Our brave kids on the front. And then what happens when you embed western media with the military? You turn journalism into a first person shooter game.

BEAR. *(To* **MARINA**.*)* Back me up here.

MARINA. I ditched my embed.

NIKKI. See!?

MARINA. The sergeant ripped me a new one. *(In a rural American accent.)* "How DARE you ditch your embed, Reyes! You are a liability to yourself, your crew, and your country. And if you cannot respect the rules we've created to safeguard this press pool then I will rip up your credentials myself and send your ass packing!"

NIKKI. And then you walked away and figured it out on your own, right?

MARINA. I mean, not on my own. There were other journalists, *(To* **BEAR**.*)* former army like you, local fixers and fighters... *(Laughs.)* The last thing that sergeant told me was to ditch my lacy bra and invest in some Kevlar.

BEAR. At least you half listened.

MARINA. And I said, "It's not lace. It's La Perla." And he said, "Good. That's how I'll know it's you if I ever dig you out of a mass grave."

NIKKI. Fucking badass.

>(**NIKKI** *raises her glass.*)

To the bygone war reporter.

MARINA. String my bones together and hang me from the ceiling in a museum.

>(*They drink.*)

>(**FED** *appears holding a bouquet of roses. Is he an illusion?*)

Fernando?

FED. Marina?

>(*No, he's real.* **BEAR** *and* **NIKKI** *leave.*)

MARINA. You came.

>(**FED** *holds out the roses. He wears a suit.*)

To be my flower girl?

FED. To win you back.

>(*Romantic music.**)

MARINA. (*To the music.*) No, stop. Stop that.

>(*The music stops.* **MARINA** *realizes she had the power to stop the music.*)

---

* A license to produce *'Til Death* does not include a performance license for any third-party or copyrighted music. Licensees should create an original composition or use music in the public domain. For further information, please see the Music and Third-Party Materials Use Note on page iii.

FED. I'm kidding.

MARINA. No you're not.

FED. Had to give it a shot. Here. Take them.

(*She takes them. She still has love for him.*)

They're actually "I'm sorry" flowers.

MARINA. Sorry for what?

FED. I gave Nikki your journals.

MARINA. You what?

FED. For the book. To use as source material.

MARINA. Book. What book? She's writing a feature. For *Vogue.*

FED. There were some pages I ripped out. I know, I know that's not good journalistic integrity on my part, but I don't know. I still feel protective over you. And I didn't want you to be completely exposed. I wanted some stuff to stay private.

And okay yeah, maybe I also did it to save my own ego. I mean, one of us still has a career here and a daughter who generally sees them in a good light... Don't need our skeletons falling out of the closet.

MARINA. The affair.

FED. "He's having an affair with one of the other moms at school. The worst part is I don't care."

MARINA. Even after that you still wanted to work things out.

FED. I have a soft spot for you.

MARINA. Sure it's not a bruise?

FED. You look okay. Better than I thought.

MARINA. My mom said the same thing.

FED. "Missing, Presumed Dead."

MARINA. I know, I know, paints a scary picture.

FED. But you look okay.

MARINA. Can't say the same for you. *(Kind of an insult.)* You wear a suit to work.

FED. It's a different kind of war.

MARINA. You really mean that.

FED. I do.

MARINA. *(Delicious.)* My god, you used to be terrifying. With your big beard and flak jacket. You'd show up in the correspondents' club and the whole room would turn to you – like kids waiting to be picked for the kickball team. Were you gonna offer a ride? Share a contact for a translator? A new smugglers' route? Terrifying.

FED. Not to you though.

MARINA. No, you walked around with that beat up copy of *The Face of War*. I thought you were adorable.

FED. Martha Gellhorn is a panty dropper.

MARINA. How many girls fell for that bullshit?

FED. A few. But there was only one I married.

MARINA. That is terrifying. And now look at you – you're fat and happy. You're happy right?

FED. I've missed you. Cruz misses you.

MARINA. Did Cruz tell you she wanted to go on tour?

FED. What? No!

MARINA. One viral video and she's practicing her Grammy acceptance speech in the shower.

FED. She's always done that. I bet it's that Tyler kid pushing that on her.

MARINA. She's done with him.

FED. Oh thank GOD. He annoyed the shit out of me. He knows that she’s in love with him and he’s just been stringing her along because he can’t make good music without her. And I couldn’t say anything or else I would get accused of trying to “break up the band.”

MARINA. So it is a band.

FED. I don’t know. It’s a kid with a laptop. Is that a band?

MARINA. …Can I ask you a crazy question?

FED. Shoot.

MARINA. Do you ever think about civil war?

FED. All the time. I’d get out of the game. Build a bunker. A nice one. Hydroponic garden. A movie theatre. I’d stockpile guns and medicine and Nespresso pods.

MARINA. What about Cruz?

FED. Tricky. She’ll be at school, and college campuses will be both / targets and hotbeds for terrorism.

MARINA. Targets and hotbeds for terrorism.

FED. She could run.

MARINA. But the second she breaks her glasses she’s fucked.

FED. She wears contacts.

MARINA. But if she had to run in the middle of the night and didn’t have time to put on her contacts.

FED. She could run during the day.

MARINA. Then she has like thirty days until they dry out.

FED. No, her optometrist switched her to dailies. I think you can only stretch those a week.

MARINA. See? Fucked.

FED. I’ll come get her. I’ll be Dennis Quaid in that apocalypse movie. Don’t worry.

MARINA. Always the Good Dad. I've missed you too.

> (**MARINA** *reaches out her hand and the romantic music starts again. They slow dance.*)

FED. You kept my name. All these years and you kept my name.

MARINA. Easier to spell. Easier to say. But I'm not yours anymore. Your name's just a head on my wall, reminding me where I've been. All the good game I've killed.

FED. And now you've caught yourself a Bear.

MARINA. Maybe this one will last.

FED. They never do.

MARINA. I have to try though. A girl's gotta eat.

I have this hunger for love and romance – weddings and puppies and babies – the safety of a life that's entirely routine.

I'm starving for it.

And then I smell it lurking nearby and I don't stop to catch my breath.

I dive in, teeth first, and feast.

But it won't stay down. It's spoiled. Poisoned.

And somehow I'm emptier than when I started.

But that starts to feel good. I'm light and quick.

The dizziness is a high to chase. The euphoria of uncertainty.

And it's anything but lonely. There's company in the hunger of others.

In the razed cities, make-shift hospitals, checkpoints, and gunfire.

…

I'm contracted to a higher power.

I stumbled into His unholy house and signed my name in blood.

> *(They stop dancing.)*

What if I have to go back?

FED. What if you do?

MARINA. Will Cruz –?

> *(She wants to say "understand" or "forgive me" but can't.)*

FED. I don't know.

> *(**CRUZ** appears as a beacon again. **MARINA** follows her.)*

CRUZ.
OH WHAT SHALL I GIVE TO THE GOD OF WAR
HE'S TAKEN MY EYE AND A PIECE OF MY BONE
AND FROM MY STOMACH THE LINING IS GONE
BUT FOR MY SLEEP HE'LL SHOW ME HIS THRONE
AMEN, AMEN MAY OUR OFFERING BE RECEIVED OH
AMEN, AMEN MAY OUR OFFERING BE RECEIVED

> *(**SONIA**, **GUMMY**, **BEAR**, **NIKKI**, *and* **FED** assemble.)*

> *(**CRUZ** joins them. They all sit.)*

> \>\>

> *(**MARINA** hovers over the empty chair meant for her. She takes a deep breath.)*

> *(**MARINA** sits.)*

(Everyone speaks all at once.)

SONIA. I knew it. There was this little voice inside me that told me not to trust this – you, the house, the wedding – I can't believe I fucking fell for it.

GUMMY. I'm so proud of what you do. I don't know if I've ever said that out loud to you, but I need you to know that buried under all my fear is pride.

CRUZ. I've been reading your journals, trying to get to know you better. But they just make me sad that we never talk. Like really talk, ya know?

NIKKI. I think there's a way to do what we do without it destroying us. I don't know. Maybe that's naive of me to say, but I have to believe it's true.

FED. We've done this enough times for me to know there's nothing I can say to stop you from doing what you want to do. I'm only here to support Cruz.

BEAR. You have to listen to them, Marina. You know I'm a bad influence. You know I'm just as fucked as you are. Look at these people, they care about you.

*(Time blinks forward as **MARINA** stands up.)*

MARINA. What if we did this a little different?

...

What if this time...

What if you all played me?

And I played you?

(They all look to each other, unsure.)

Will you indulge me? Please?

(No one objects.)

Who wants to go first?

  (**SONIA** *stands, but doesn't know where to start.*)

You're me. I'm you. Why don't you start with what you thought I was gonna say here.

SONIA. Well I knew you weren't gonna stay home.

MARINA. No, but say it pretending you're me.

SONIA. *(Still uncertain.)* You knew I wasn't gonna stay.

MARINA. *(Snapping expertly into the roleplay.)* Of course I knew, FUCKING FEMININE INTUITION.

  (**SONIA** *is taken aback.* **MARINA** *takes this incredibly seriously and is very good at expressing* **SONIA**'s *perspective without ever mocking it – it challenges* **SONIA** *to do the same.*)

SONIA. *(Still unsure.)* It's my job… Sonia.

MARINA. It's not a job, it's a death wish!

SONIA. *(This is harder than she thought.)* I don't believe that.

MARINA. Of course you don't, you're delusional!

SONIA. But… I'm still capable of making my own decisions.

MARINA. You're not! Clinically speaking! You're not capable! You don't have the executive function for it!

SONIA. *(Slowly getting the hang of it.)* You don't get to diagnose me.

MARINA. Your brain is fucking fried, Marina! Please, let us help you!

SONIA. I've tried therapy.

MARINA. You'll try again.

SONIA. And I have to keep working.

MARINA. No you don't!

SONIA. *(Biting back.)* Yes I do! I'm broke! I've always been terrible with money. You of all people should know that!

MARINA. Sell this fucking house! Or tell me who to write a check to!

SONIA. *(More to herself.)* You can't throw money at all your problems, Sonia!

MARINA. Watch me!

SONIA. And I...like what I do! I believe in it! What kind of example am I setting for Cruz if I quit?

MARINA. What kind of example are you setting if you're dead?

SONIA. At least it will have meant something!

MARINA. It's not fair that you get to be selfish and still stand on moral high ground. It's not fair that we're all just collateral damage to your higher calling. And I know it's a higher calling. But it's also an addiction, Marina. It's also just fucking chemicals swirling around in your body. And it's not fair that I'm not enough. That your mother isn't enough. That Cruz isn't enough. It's not fair that the only blood you care about is a stranger's.

SONIA. You know that's not true – *(Breaking.)* You know I don't think that, right?

MARINA. *(Breaking.)* Please, stay in it.

SONIA. *(Searching for a way back into the roleplay.)* I love you... Sonia. I love all of you. I know my actions might not always show that, but I'm not trying to hurt you.

MARINA. We just want you to stay home.

SONIA. I can't.

MARINA. It's easy! It's the easiest thing you could do!

SONIA. You don't get it!

MARINA. Get what?!

> (**SONIA** *works hard to put herself in* **MARINA**'s *shoes, and really discovers in the moment what it must be like to be her.*)

SONIA. Even when I'm here with you, I'm still over there. I'm always still over there. It's like you always say, trauma on trauma on trauma. A car backfires and I can taste blood in my mouth and my lungs fill up with ash. Someone spills wine and all I can see is the kid wailing in the back of a pickup truck trying to keep his leg attached to the rest of his body. I've just seen too much. I think there's a limit on how much a person can see in a lifetime and I've surpassed that. And I'm not sleeping. Maybe this would all be easier if I could sleep. But I'm reporting live from fucking nightmare land where I have to break the story. Everyone is expecting me to break the story. And I wake up drenched in sweat and come out here into my pretty green garden and all of it has turned grey.

MARINA. *(Deathly.)* So how could you even think of going back?

SONIA. *(A quick and painful revelation.)* Because at least there the grey makes sense.

> (**SONIA** *has surprised herself with that answer and takes a seat.*)

> (**MARINA** *looks to everyone else.*)

> (**GUMMY** *stands. She holds Marina's veil.*)

GUMMY. I wanna go.

MARINA. Okay.

GUMMY. But I'm not roleplaying.

MARINA. Mom –

GUMMY. I'm not roleplaying.

MARINA. Fine. What are you doing with my veil?

GUMMY. *(Unsentimental.)* Jazzing it up. The lace appliqué is from my mother's dress.

MARINA. *(Suddenly embarrassed.)* I'm sorry, Mom. I'm sorry we have to do this again.

GUMMY. Don't with the "I'm sorry"s.

MARINA. I mean it.

GUMMY. I don't accept your apology. You don't owe me one.

MARINA. Yes I do.

GUMMY. I thought you did. For a long time. I thought you only did all this to punish me.

MARINA. What?

GUMMY. For living, you know, the way I lived. The boyfriends and the occasional disappearances.

MARINA. Mom –

GUMMY. And for believing in God. You always made me feel stupid for that, so I thought you went over there to prove to me he doesn't exist.

MARINA. Mom –

GUMMY. Let me finish this because I've had a lot of time to think about it. I owe *you* the apology. For all the years I've spent mourning you. Treating you like the walking dead. Since the Sapphire. Since the kidnapping. Since the thing in Syria. I've buried you so many times in my mind I've lost track. And sometimes – I'm sorry – but sometimes I wish you'd just stay buried. Because it's just too painful, Marina. Too painful. So I'm sorry. I'm sorry for wishing that.

(**GUMMY** *takes a seat.*)

(**MARINA** *takes a deep breath and braces herself. Everyone looks to* **CRUZ.**)

MARINA. Cruz. Do you want to say anything?

(**CRUZ** *has an unusually sunny demeanor.*)

CRUZ. You're late!

MARINA. What?

(**CRUZ** *stands up and starts pushing* **MARINA** *off.*)

CRUZ. Go! You're supposed to be getting dressed!

MARINA. Cruz –

CRUZ. Come on!

MARINA. The award?

CRUZ. No! That never mattered.

MARINA. What –?

CRUZ. Come on! You're running out of time!

MARINA. Wait!

CRUZ. Go! All of you!

(**CRUZ** *claps everyone into action.* **SONIA** *escorts a confused* **MARINA** *off. Everyone else leaves knowing exactly where to go.*)

(*Only* **CRUZ** *is left. She remains sunny.*)

You know, I've imagined your funeral a million times, but never your wedding. Don't worry, it's gorgeous. *Vogue* could never. And the whole thing is like super sad, but not surprising sad – more like, a satisfying sad. Like when you pick up a book and you know it's a tragedy, but you still let yourself get swept up by the end – and you're crying, but you're also kind of amazed 'cause now all the tiny details have finally been revealed and they all perfectly click into place and deliver an ending that your brain knew was coming, but now finally reaches your heart.

(**MARINA** *appears in her wedding dress.*)

(**CRUZ** *beams at her.*)

(*This is light and tender, through loving smiles.*)

You look beautiful, Mom.

MARINA. *(The painful truth.)* I'm dying, right?

CRUZ. You are.

MARINA. I never made it home.

CRUZ. It's okay. I'll be okay.

MARINA. Are you sure?

CRUZ. You're not gone. You're in my music.

(*They hug.*)

MARINA. It's not too much? The wedding?

CRUZ. No, Mom, you deserve a happy ending.

BEAR. *(From offstage.)* Marina!

MARINA. *(Shouting offstage.)* You're not supposed to see me in my dress!

CRUZ. It's okay, Mom, go. I'll see you.

MARINA. Cruz, everyone always wondered how I could leave you again and again. And when I was pregnant I wondered too. How could I leave you? I thought I had to prove you wouldn't change me. Stayed in the field a little too long. At one point I couldn't feel you move anymore. So my fixer drove six hours straight to get me to an army hospital. The whole time I was crying where are you? Where are you? Where are you? And there you were. Early, but alive. My guts spilled out on the table and I thought they forgot to put my heart back inside, 'cause there you were carrying it. You carry my heart. And when I go back in the field that's all I can see, all these little hearts. And I know I can stay 'cause my heart is safe at home.

CRUZ. Mom –

MARINA. Promise me, Cruz, promise you'll keep my heart safe.

CRUZ. I promise! Now go, you're late!

MARINA. It's my party. I'm just in time.

>   (*The* Vogue *wedding! Flowers! Lights! Decor! The string quartet! Everyone is in their garden formal attire.*)

>   (**MARINA** *meets* **BEAR** *in his tux at the altar.*)

I'll have you.

BEAR. I'll hold you.

MARINA. I'll cherish you.

BEAR. I'll honor you.

MARINA. I'll love you.

BEAR. I'll carry you.

MARINA. I love you.

BEAR. I'll carry your body.

>   (**MARINA** *looks out to her friends and family.*)

MARINA. You'll take care of her, right? You'll take care of my girl?

(They all breathe together.)

MARINA. Thank you.

*(**MARINA** and **BEAR** kiss.)*

(An iconic dance song starts to play. By Candi Staton, ABBA, or Earth, Wind & Fire... something you can't help but dance in your seat to.)*

(Confetti falls all around them.)

*(**MARINA** and **BEAR** walk hand in hand in pure bliss through the wedding party and off out of sight.)*

(The party dances. It's fully choreographed. Infectiously joyful.)

(It's getting brighter.)

(You're probably dancing in your seat now too.)

(Soon your eyes start to squint as the stage becomes a big blinding white light. It's so bright.)

(Then suddenly it's like someone pulls out the plug. The music and stage lights go out. Then the house and work lights come up abruptly. It almost feels like an accident. Before our eyes can adjust, we hear him.)

BEAR. HEEEELP! HEEEEELP!! HEEEEEELP!!!

---

* A license to produce *'Til Death* does not include a performance license for any third-party or copyrighted music. Licensees should create an original composition or use music in the public domain. For further information, please see the Music and Third-Party Materials Use Note on page iii.

(**MARINA** *is laying on the ground, in her flak jacket and helmet bleeding.* **BEAR** *is kneeling over her body. They're alone. The whole stage is covered in ash.*)

HEEELP! HEEEELP!

(**BEAR** *starts to carry her body off.*)

JOURNALIST! JOURNALIST! HEEEEELP! JOURNALIST!

(**BEAR** *and* **MARINA** *are gone. For half a second we stare at the naked stage.*)

(**CRUZ** *enters like a beacon once more. The lights softly restore to the world of the play. Somewhere in a place of eternal peace and absolution.*)

CRUZ.
WHAT SHALL I GIVE TO THE GOD OF WAR
WHEN ALL THE INVISIBLE PARTS OF ME FADE
NO MUSIC OR LAUGHTER OR DAYDREAMS REMAIN
AFTER MY SOUL, WHAT ELSE DO I TRADE?
AMEN, AMEN, MAY OUR OFFERING BE RECEIVED
AMEN, AMEN, MAY OUR OFFERING BE RECEIVED

(*Blackout.*)

End of Play

www.ingramcontent.com/pod-product-compliance
Lightning Source LLC
Chambersburg PA
CBHW070644120726
47909CB00004B/1567